Read*ux*

Readux Books: Series 1, № 3

Originally published as *Fantasy*
by Novellix, Stockholm

First English translation, 2013

ISBN: 978-3-944801-02-5

Cover illustration by André Gottschalk
Design by Susann Stefanizen

Published by Readux Books
Sorauer Str. 16, 10997 Berlin, Germany

www.readux.net

Fantasy

Malte Persson
Translated from the Swedish by Saskia Vogel

The whisper of castles in the sky collapsing. (Insert special effects here.) The drag force of passing deadlines and overdrawn budgets. Was it all just a matter of money, as usual? Or was there, as some say, another story, better insofar as it was much worse? I'm not much for conspiracy theories, but I am fascinated by money: numbers made from a void that we use as a synonym for reality. Is there a worse conspiracy? I said this to the Sorrowful Prince, who seemed to understand what I meant. He was an intelligent person in many ways, one whose money had wrapped him in an unreality that he unsuccessfully tried to reshape into something he could live with. He was the first one to tell me about *The Plot*. Though it had been covered by the media, it was already forgotten. The Sorrowful Prince told me too much, but it was far from everything. His official perspective was, of course, that everything was just a matter of money.

The Plot, if it had been made, would have been an utterly lavish film by Swedish standards. There was a script based on a hitherto unpublished short story by the latest Swedish literary star in the hottest genre after crime fiction: fantasy. We can (with or without a straight face) call him the Witch Master, like some newspapers did, at least before the most recent tragedies. There was a director, with a few well-received but modest films to his name. For him the project seemed to be The Big Test—potentially his portal to Hollywood, another world. We can call him Anonymous, because he'll never make a name for himself. There was an actress being considered for the female lead, young and beautiful, who we can call the Protagonist. There was an actor being considered for the male lead, young and beautiful, who we can call the Antagonist. Naturally, there was an extremely competent producer, who I will keep even more anonymous than everyone else. There were promises of financial backing from the powers that be, in other words State and Capital. The latter word is a bit misleading, because there was namely one individual who had already sunk a few million into the project before it was shut down. In the press, he was usually referred to as "the young IT-genius" and the like. But I want to call him the Sorrowful Prince, because that was how I, with varying degrees of irony and sarcasm, thought of him after we met. There were a bunch of others involved; I'd especially like to mention the one I just have to call the Dwarf. Not for his stature, but because of his underground habits and gift for craftsmanship. (On the internet forums he frequents, he picked a user name that references the crafty dwarves of the Icelandic sagas. I can't go into it more than that.) I thought of the Dwarf as my main character. He was the only one who hadn't put the wreck of a project behind him. For him money was less of a concern. His conspiracy was the only one that, on closer consideration, was even greater. I mean: language.

I think this is a story about language, but I'm not sure. I met the Sorrowful Prince by chance, in a bar—it doesn't matter which. I was one of the many potential princesses he bought drinks for. It ended with me following him home. Not because he was a type I'm interested in. But because he was the type whose stories interest me. He lived in what I found to be a dreary but dear, hi-tech attic apartment a short taxi-ride away, where everything was connected to everything else via cables, bluetooth, wi-fi, dust, and spider webs. Shadows crept fuzzily in the corners. I assume he didn't see it as his job to clean, or to let anyone else in to do it. The electronics, on or on stand-by, gave off a pale blue glow that was the opposite of cozy. He had to take a computer off the unmade bed before we could have sex. (I said: "There's room for all three of us, if you like.") Our first coupling was not-unpleasant foreplay to our verbal intercourse.

Making others believe that they are using me and not vice versa has always been a talent of mine. Or perhaps my talent is convincing myself of this, and not vice versa. In any case: my stories are always parasites on others' stories. "A fly on the wall," as they say in the language of reportage. There are fly-like surveillance drones now, I have learned… Me, I am a big fucking irritating fly, one who annoys people in their bedrooms on a late summer night when they're trying to sleep with the window open. The kind that—tadah!—always has its little digital camera on hand to capture the things that are there to catch. And for me, as for other flies, witnessing someone's defeat is material that is as good as, or more nourishing than witnessing a victory. Ha, just listen to me buzz. The record-light shines in my favorite hue, redder than blood and the first May Day protest. Or whatever.

It bears mentioning that I have never cared about fantasy. That which we call fiction has never been my department. Reality is what interests me, I usually say. Documented reality, I should say as a documentary film artist (not the kind who degrades herself by pitching ideas to Swedish public television, but one who is at home in the absurdity of the art world). And the attraction for me in this was precisely the victory of reality over fantasy. People talk about reality like it's something fixed, but to me it's ever-malleable. So flexible, compared to the static constructions of fantasy. So boundless. The Sorrowful Prince may have been an expert in computer simulations, but no algorithm or fractal can create anything that can measure up to the real's infinite, endlessly layered, and constantly shifting textures. Okay, I'll stop before I start sounding like a project proposal or catalog copy. But so far, I do believe what I'm saying. "You have only scratched the surface," the Dwarf said dryly to me later. But this is also what distinguishes the surfaces of reality: that they can weather being scratched.

So... after I heard the Sorrowful Prince talk about *The Plot*, I Googled it and found the rumors. There was a thread in a forum, which spoke of mysterious threats: those involved are said to have had unusual symbols carved into their doors, and so on. Someone who knew someone. None of it could be confirmed, but even stories about a story can be part of the story, I think. Of course the discussion quickly got out of hand, as nerds, trolls and other internet creatures hurled accusations at one another. The usual conspiracy theorists tried to link the alleged events to the usual global conspiracies: Muslims, Jews, aliens, new world order. All this suited me well. I thought: material.

I'll admit that I'm fascinated by dreams that have crashed and shattered, or at least cracked. It has to do with my upbringing, which I'm not going to get into here. It's enough that I continue to be the spoiled art-school chick, the privileged, pretty, family-financed brat, a cliché with perfect skin, for whom no doors are locked, in principle, but who still never gets any further than the stairwell. But heaven knows stairwells can be interesting places. (Note to self: totally different project: everything I have done in stairwells, concrete, symbolic, etc., etc.)

Reality: people like to convince themselves that it exists somewhere else. In the suburbs. In nature. Somewhere out there, in any case, outside the skin. That is, if they aren't dumb enough to believe that it exists deep inside: in the soul, the heart, sexuality, whatever. I think the only true reality is the surface: my view of the world, the world's view of me, I explained to each of them. "The interface," said the Sorrowful Prince. "Language," said the Dwarf. Good boys! But to dedicate yourself to a fictional language…?

Honestly I don't know what won over what in the end, and my project (working title: *Fantasy*) was as unfinished as theirs. And the worst thing is that this sorrowful fucking tone—that's theirs, not mine, but I'm aware of it anyway—tries to creep into my own account of everything. It's so not me! But it's stuck in my head, and to, well, purge it… I'm telling their story. And I'll be done soon, I hope: I'm certainly not going to say everything, just enough. Then I'll see what I'll do with the memory card. Delete or save, an existential choice as good as any, right?

There's a tinge of a reality TV confessional about this project, I say as an aside. I've already gotten rid of the other recordings. But anyway, finding the others involved—those who weren't melancholics and failed romantics—was a breath of fresh air. The Witch Master turned out to be a banal character, thankfully. I've met them before, men who've found success ten or fifteen years after they started going after it full-time, and who now desperately try to squeeze as much out of it as possible. Those who, for example, start doing cocaine at an age when the rest of us have long since stopped. And not to mention the sex. But, what the hell, maybe he was within his rights, considering what little time he had left to live. His success was validated in spades. To be found tied up and drained of blood in your newly renovated bathroom can do wonders for a book's print run, even one that was large to begin with. As for his dignity, that was already lost. But who am I to etc., etc.

In any case: he happily let me interview him, and babbled on about himself, but didn't have much worthwhile to say about the story I was interested in. The story that was supposed to have been turned into the film was an extension of his "fictional universe," he said. (Dork.) It was about a struggle for power between those with fairy blood and those with troll blood—the former being very beautiful, ice-cold psychopaths occupying leading roles in society, and the latter nocturnal charmers and commodity speculators in the underworld. Terribly corny, at least broken down like this, but I didn't say that, of course.

He didn't really know why the film wasn't made, but it wasn't particularly unusual, and did I know, by the way, just how well he was paid for the rights?

He clumsily tried to seduce me later, but he didn't have a shot. Nevertheless, I read a couple of his books "as research" (he foisted a few copies on me that he signed with embarrassing dedications), and even if that kind of writing isn't my thing, I have to admit, they weren't bad. This genre, "Sture Square Fantasy," that he came up with, was in itself a sure success. Alternate dimensions, stock brokers without reflections, secret rooms behind the O Bar that you don't return from, not to this Stockholm, but to another Stockholm, darker and more dangerous, where feudal clans fight for power... *Easy Money* meets *Narnia*, in short. But aside from that, there was something I-don't-know-what. So maybe I should have called him the Golden Goose instead of the Witch Master. Because, once you start laying golden eggs, it's only a matter of time until someone breaks your neck.

Even open-plan apartments can conceal secrets. There is a darkness in the pale, the white. The Scandinavian Gothic? The midnight sun, which has to be recompensed during another season. I'm reading from my notes, but it's unclear what's a quotation and what my own thoughts are.

I never got a hold of Anonymous. Me and everyone else. The closest I got was his mother, who informed me from her apartment in the suburbs that he wasn't interested in speaking with me. I moved on. The beautiful young Antagonist had, in contrast to Anonymous, disappeared to Hollywood. I tried to trick his agent into thinking I was Sofia Coppola and had a part to offer him, but maybe that was a bit far-fetched and it didn't go anywhere. Later, I saw him in a worthless vampire movie where he got to have sex with Amanda Seyfried. According to what I heard from acquaintances who had run into him, he was a completely uninteresting person, but so are most actors when there isn't anyone around to direct them. And a pig, but so are most men who've figured out that they can get away with it. The only thing I underlined in a number of interviews with him in newspapers from recent years was the following quotation: "Most people would do anything to be successful. I do almost anything. You wouldn't believe me if I told you what I haven't done." Similarly: "People think Sweden is a good country. It isn't. I don't know what I would have

14

done if that wasn't where I came from." But later he quotes Ayn Rand, so you shouldn't take what he says too seriously.

I did get in touch with the beautiful female Protagonist, however. She was doing Chekhov at the City Theater, and it turned out we had met before, at an art school party a while ago. We had a few glasses of wine at the Artists' Bar and had a pleasant evening, but she laughed away the story of *The Plot*. She said it wasn't a given that she would have gotten the lead.

"The exact circumstances don't matter," said the Sorrowful Prince, "but everything was delayed and the other private backers pulled out. And contrary to what some people believe, my assets aren't inexhaustible."

They must have been reasonably large in any case. The Sorrowful Prince worked for "the dark side." Those were his words. "The biggest sell-out since Saruman allied himself with Sauron," he said. His company had developed unique software that simulated and analyzed group behavior during conflicts. Populations, armies, social movements. In the beginning he thought it might be used for computer games, various kinds of realistic strategy games. Then he became fascinated with the project's inherent possibilities and allowed himself to get carried away. It ended up being bought for a fantastical sum by an American company, that, he only found out later, had some sort of connection to Academi, formerly Xe, formerly Blackwater (Google as needed), and which could, who knows, use it as part of their consultancy for who knows which warlords and dictators. Everything would have been okay if he could have just taken the money and run, but he was contractually obligated to stay on another five years and continue to head up development. As is customary under these circumstances.

So, that's why he was what he was now: the Sorrowful Prince captive in his castle and in his realm. The Sorrowful Prince with his nerdy cocktail orders, which, more often than not, he had to explain to the bartender. The Sorrowful Prince watching *Lord of the Rings* on Blu-Ray in his home cinema. The Sorrowful Prince listening to Bat for Lashes on his ridiculously expensive stereo system. (Me, I'm more a Mozart and house girl.)

In spite of everything, I liked him. I recognized the cognitive dissonance present in the best in the art world: those who didn't deny the appeal of cynical, empty competition, but at the same time preserved enough of their ideals to recognize and hate that emptiness.

The Plot was what would have justified the Sorrowful Prince's dubiously earned fortune. Anything for art!

I told him that reading more Nietzsche would do him good.

Okay, I haven't talked about the producer. I won't talk about the producer. If I had talked with the producer, which I'm not suggesting I have, then the producer made it clear that I shouldn't talk about the producer.

Apropos nothing, law is also something that fascinates me. The law fills the same ostensibly reality-shaping function as money. And don't get me started on the insurance sector, with its fictions and alternate realities—not dealing in truth, but in probability. Just as in Aristotle's book on tragedy, which is popular in Hollywood, too. Yes, I'm well-read. I've attended the odd university course. In case you thought otherwise. Anyway: money, laws, and insurance are all important in film production, of course. And if, purely hypothetically, a highly influential person or group should want to stop a film production, then it's not like you have

to make mysterious threats or engineer a spectac-
ular death for a famous author. No peripeteia.

One more thing about the Witch-Master-slash-
Golden-Goose. Someone tipped me off that for a
while (before he became successful), he had jotted
down aphorisms on a Twitter account that almost
no one followed. Shreds of ideas, like: "When the
dead arise, they'll do it on Facebook." Or more
laughably: "'The medium is the message,' said the
parapsychologist." And so on. I don't know if this is
on point. I don't even know if it was him. It doesn't
really sound like him, but people can change.

But back to language. The Sorrowful Prince
introduced me to the Dwarf, who was an old
schoolmate. Partners in nerd-dom at some high
school around the godforsaken turn of the millen-
nium. But whereas the Prince had been capti-
vated by programming languages, the Dwarf had
been drawn to regular languages. Well, regular
and regular. It wasn't like he was interested in
conversing while on holiday or making a career
as an interpreter for the EU. He mainly learned
dead languages and constructed languages—Elvish,
Klingon, you know. Languages that you can avoid
speaking, except maybe sometimes with other

like-minded nerds. He did have a great talent for this hobby. It never became more than a hobby. He had tried to study classical comparative linguistics at university, but the institute shut down shortly after he started. He harbored hatred for Noam Chomsky, whom he claimed had destroyed the last fifty years of acdemic linguistics with his "pseudo-scientific shortcuts that never led anywhere." (His friend the Prince agreed on this point, but they fell out over something about Google Translate, which may have been uncontaminated by Chomsky's generative grammar, but still used "unsportsmanlike statistical analysis," according to the Dwarf.) I tried to get him to change the subject. And if he had really enjoyed the university milieu, he could have just moved to another city or to another country.

So, languages remained a hobby, alongside board games and the like, until, thanks to the Prince, he became involved in *The Plot*. Since the heyday of *Star Trek*, constructed languages in film and television had become an increasingly elaborate field. As much attention was now paid to language as to clothing. (As an aside, one could wish that people in general, those in the center of Stockholm for instance, did too.) Consequently, experts were hired to create believable languages for everything from the dopey blue-screen-blue aborigines in *Avatar* to the pornographic desert plunderers in *Game of Thrones*. And why should we do any worse in Sweden?

For copyright reasons, you couldn't adopt Tolkien's Elvish, the Dwarf explained, which would have otherwise been a simple solution. But its structure could still provide the foundation—the new language could be in relation to Tolkien's Elvish as Swedish is to Icelandic, for instance. Yet the Dwarf, language nerd that he was, didn't want to simplify the grammar too much. Elvish, at least the kind that's called *Quenya*, I think, was already influenced by Finnish, so it made sense to link it back to the Nordic. The Dwarf added cognates from Tornedal-Finnish and North Sami, but also borrowed the grammar from another one of Tolkien's Elvish languages that was more influenced by Indo-European languages, to which he (for his own amusement) added Indo-European influences that Tolkien couldn't have been aware of, namely Hittite. Etc., etc. And then there was the troll language, too: a guttural and paratactic pidgin with a scant vocabulary for everything but insults, sex, and economics. He could talk about this endlessly, and he soon lost me, but I let the camera roll.

I couldn't help thinking his interest in language was totally misguided, but that's exactly why I found it fascinating. By the way, I know I use the word "fascinating" too much. I once asked the Dwarf how you would say it in his Sture Square Elvish, and he said the closest synonym he had was the word for "bewitch."

We chatted about language a few times. He said that the first word he learned as a child was "lamp," which apparently was normal. He speculated that the children who learned this word first ran a greater risk of being lonely people. I told him that my first word was the name of an au-pair girl we had when my family lived in Paris for a few years when I was little. (She took me for walks on the Champs-Élysées, just like in Proust.) I also mentioned that I had an acquaintance who was pleased that his daughter's first word was "dad," until he realized that she actually meant "pad," as in iPad, her favorite toy.

The Dwarf said that this could be a new Grimm tale: the prince who was turned into an iPad. I said nothing. Obviously I hadn't mentioned to either the Prince or the Dwarf that I thought of them as the Prince and the Dwarf, respectively.

The Dwarf went on to talk about the achievements of the Brothers Grimm as linguists. I listened politely. You can call me Snow White.

I assume the Prince continued to finance his language-making in some way, but I didn't ask. Money talks, I said. But what language does it speak? Can you construct that language? A constructed language seemed to me to be as meaningful as creating your own currency or printing your own bank notes. The Sorrowful Prince had explained that creating one's own currency was more than a philosophical experiment. He reminded me that online role-playing games like *World of Warcraft* have their own exchangeable currencies. That there are Chinese sweatshops where low-wage employees mine the fictional gold in the game, and then sell it for real dollars to players in the West. And he showed me an article in the *Financial Times*, or maybe it was the *Economist*, about how a mobile phone company in Kenya created its own digital currency that was on its way to being as widely used as the country's official currency. There were more examples. Bitcoin and what not. I asked him if he was thinking of devoting himself to this in the future. He shrugged. He was convinced that the financial system would collapse, like the fiction that it was, and he had a backup of actual gold stored "in a safe place." That made me smile. The Sorrowful Prince and his hidden treasure.

The Dwarf also shrugged at my pointless questions.

We met a few times at a cafe, an old-fashioned place near a market square in the suburbs, meat-ball sandwiches and pale faces and oily coffee with free refills. I usually prefer to meet people in their homes, for the atmosphere and because it's calmer, but the Dwarf's… den… felt too claustrophobic. It was a basement flat with a low ceiling and books everywhere, and the same kind of spider webs as in the Sorrowful Prince's… castle… but even more of them, and of course in a smaller space. Even more shadows, and with sharper edges. I never saw any spiders, or did I? Something vague just outside my field of vision. Anyway, it made me dream about them. Black and big and fast, and more and more from night to night. I don't know if this is relevant.

Obviously I know things don't exist just because you see them. What you sense out of the corner of your eye isn't anything more than scratches on an old film print or compression artifacts in a jpeg. And vice-versa: just because you don't see something doesn't mean it isn't there. In one of my earlier art projects, I (just like al-Qaeda and Behring Breivik and other epigones) worked with secret messages encrypted in image files. I didn't sell the pictures, but rather the password to the pictures. It then was the duty of the prospective collector to keep the password secret so his investment wouldn't become worthless. Okay, we're getting sidetracked, and I can't say I made much money from this, but it was a good idea anyway.

Somewhere I read that what is understood as "realism" in a literary work is directly related to how much of the work in question is about money. Which is nonsense, I suppose. Money is a product of fantasy that produces new products of fantasy. It would be more correct to say that realism is a question of a lack of money. But what do I know about that?

Anyhow, I'm not afraid of contradicting myself. There are—here comes an understatement!—much worse things to be afraid of. I try to go by feeling, and so on. I try ideas out. I have a special mind-mapping program on my computer. (An iMac with a 24-inch display, loaded with unique hacking software. Nah, just kidding. Lisbeth-fucking-Salander I ain't. But I can point and click. And a little more.) After a while, a mind-map also looks like a kind of spider web, and it's easy to get tangled in too many ideas.

The word fantasy is from the Greek *phainestai*, "to appear," which, similar to *phos*, "light," has its roots in an Indo-European free morpheme that sounded something like "bha" and had something to do with shining. The Dwarf taught me. It has nothing to do with *fan* (the devil) or elephants. "In practice, fantasy is a question of realism," asserted the Dwarf. Clearly, he had thought about this. "That's why Tolkien is the master. His world is constructed in such detail that it feels all-encompassing. So you escape seeing the reality between the stitches…"

Tolkien's web is so tightly woven that you don't even notice what's clearly missing: sex and religion. Personally, I find this stifling. I have forced myself to watch the movies, as research, but I didn't get past Bilbo's fucking birthday party in the book. The Dwarf said that he had had several objections

25

to the new Swedish translation of *The Lord of the Rings*, even if it was much better than the old version, and also had written to the translator about this. The translator sent a polite reply.

The Dwarf also wrote a lot of emails to me, which I answered with polite and succinct evasion. I felt a bit guilty, because he had a crush on me, of course. Or to be frank: as usual, I only felt that I should have felt a bit guilty, without actually feeling it. Meta-guilt is as close as I get to that kind of regret. The derivation of a bad conscience. (If I were inclined to have a really bad conscience, I might even regret that I chose to call him the Dwarf. But I don't.)

Nonetheless he was my favorite person in this story. Talking to the Prince had always been an entertaining challenge, a mutual probing and parrying, followed by personal confidences after the other had withstood the test. But with the Dwarf I didn't have to be on my guard in the same way. He was clearly so happy that someone like me wanted to listen. And as uninterested as I was in many of the things that interested him, I was still deeply interested by the fact that he was so interested. The point, if I may be banal, was that talking with him was easy and fun.

But perhaps not forever, of course.

The last time I saw the Dwarf was a month ago, but he's sent more emails since then. We spoke about language, mainly. He taught me that there are cultures with special languages that are used when women speak with each other. He taught me that, about every other week, somewhere on earth a language dies. All of which interested me in one way or another. For reasons I won't get into, to the extent that's they're not apparent, I had already decided to stop working on my project. For the same reasons that made me undertake this symbolic and childish fairy-tale-like anonymization. Yes, I have changed many other facts too, but it's just too easy to identify those involved. Or better said, it would be, if, purely hypothetically, my project were based on anything real at all. Which, if anyone asks, I will of course deny. As it usually says at the start of the film: "All characters appearing in this work are fictitious. Any resemblance to real persons, living or dead, is purely coincidental." (Living or dead, hmm?) By the way, do people do anything but write books about real people nowadays and, if anyone complains, insist that it was only a novel, and what can you say to that? A cynical act in the margin of error between certain truth and certain fiction. Between the real real and the real unreal. Or just between suspension of disbelief and deniability.

But whatever. As I've suggested, most of the Dwarf's social contacts came from the web, where he communicated in obscure forums for the like-minded and even kept a relatively hidden blog. He seemed to be happy with this limited publicity. He approached the Witch Master's constructed world with the same unusually grave seriousness as other constructed worlds, but he didn't want to comment on the author's death, nor on the rumors about the whole thing, more than an "I don't know," or a "What do I know." The Prince, the Dwarf said, always kept him at arm's length from the others involved, and that didn't bother him. But once he uttered: "You've only scratched the surface." And I thought that maybe I had completely misjudged him. But I let it go, and soon he was his usual one-dimensional self again. He brushed off the fact that the production was shut down. "I have my languages that I've begun," he said, "and those, like all languages, can never be complete. They are or they make their own reality. And that is something I intend to pursue.

That's enough. If the film had been made, it would have only contained fragments of it anyway."

I can't help but wish that I could enjoy my work in the same way. It still irritates me that I exerted myself unnecessarily. But in the short run it doesn't matter because I got dumped by my gallerist the other day anyway. I can't say it was unexpected. He's a shit-talking predator. But well, I'm a scavenger and no stranger to shit, so maybe it'll work out this time, too. Like before.

Okay, cut, or whatever you say. That is, this meaningless talk, as well as my last contact with those involved. The Sorrowful Prince has gone away, "on business," and we parted amicably. The Dwarf, for his part, wrote to me again a few days ago. He seemed upset. Someone had contacted him with a message, flawlessly written, in his own constructed Elvish. Someone who wanted to meet. A *fan*, I said offhand and encouragingly: someone who read your blog, maybe a kindred spirit? Because what else could it be?

BERLIN - THE SLOW WAY

In the same way that the Slow Food revolution has created a compelling antithesis to the burgeoning Fast Food business, Slow Travel encourages people to resist "Fast" Travel – the frustratingly frequent habit of speeding through all the best known landmarks of a city in 24 or 48 hours – then leaving again. Slow Travel encourages us to slacken our pace, re-consider our motivations (and itineraries) and embrace a "less is more" instead of a "fast is better" ethos. It emboldens us to take pause. To think. To saunter instead of rush and enjoy the details instead of blurring past them.

We aim to facilitate any quest to get beneath the skin of the city a little, or discover it at a more leisurely pace. We offer an insider's view that will doubtless overlap from time to time with other Berlin travel sites, but will ultimately provide a unique and above all reliable resource that gives a broader, deeper perspective. We love this city and we want you to love it too.

www.slowtravelberlin.com

Malte Persson

Malte Persson, born 1976 in Mora, Sweden, is among the most significant Swedish authors of his generation. He works as an author, critic, and translator. His debut novel, *Life on This Planet*, appeared in 2002. His second novel, *Edelcrantz*, was nominated for the prestigious August Prize. He has published three volumes of poetry, including the critically acclaimed *Underworld*, a sonnet cycle about the Stockholm subway. He has won a number of awards, both for his work as an author and as a critic, including the *Gothenburg Post*'s 2011 prize for literature, whose jury praised him for "authorship that demonstrates the playfulness of a trickster, and elegant craftsmanship that reveals new worlds between earth, moon, and underworld." His most recent work is the children's book *The Journey to the World's Most Dangerous Country*. After living for many years in Stockholm, Persson now resides in Berlin.